T0380717

Gentle Whispers
From My Heavenly Father

Gentle Whispers
From My Heavenly Father

Inspirational Stories, Thoughts, and Commentaries

BECKY BYRD

WESTBOW
PRESS®
A DIVISION OF THOMAS NELSON
& ZONDERVAN

WestBow Press books may be ordered through booksellers or by contacting:

WestBow Press
A Division of Thomas Nelson & Zondervan
1663 Liberty Drive
Bloomington, IN 47403
www.westbowpress.com
844-714-3454

All Scripture taken from the King James Version of the Bible.

ISBN: 979-8-3850-2737-8 (sc)
ISBN: 979-8-3850-2738-5 (hc)
ISBN: 979-8-3850-2739-2 (e)

Library of Congress Control Number: 2024912046

Print information available on the last page.

WestBow Press rev. date: 9/13/2024

CONTENTS

ACKNOWLEDGMENTS

I would like to thank my friend Sharon for all the days of editing and emotional support. Thanks to my friend Lesley for last-minute editing, and her advice on footnotes.

Thanks to all my friends for their encouragement. Thanks to the Lord for guiding me to write these stories, as they are Holy Spirit–inspired.

May God bless everyone who has had a part in this effort, and may God bless those who read it.

INTRODUCTION

Over many years I have heard my heavenly Father speak to my heart. As I have listened to His voice, I began to write things down. The thoughts, insights, stories, and commentaries you are about to read are some of the things God has given to me.

I never knew when I would hear His voice, or what He would say, but I was always impressed to write them down. Sometimes I would hear a message on the radio, and something that was said struck a chord in my heart. Sometimes, as I studied a Bible lesson, a verse would jump out at me and speak God's message. There have been times I was praying, and God suddenly spoke something to me; I immediately had to go write it down. There have even been times I saw something, and God's Spirit would bring a scriptural illustration to my mind. I never knew when these things would come, but when they did, I knew they were from my heavenly Father.

God speaks to His children all the time. and we need to be listening so we can hear Him. I have been listening, hearing, and writing these messages for many years. I have saved them up, waiting for the time God was ready for me to pass them on. Now is that time.

I hope you will enjoy reading these writings. As you read, I pray that God's Holy Spirit will speak to your heart as He has to mine. I pray you will receive new insight for your life, and that you will draw closer to your heavenly Father. So enjoy reading—but remember to listen as God whispers a message for you. I pray you will receive it!

Becky Byrd

Gentle Whispers
From My Heavenly Father

1. God's Rooms of Knowledge and Wisdom

I SAW IN A DREAM a door that led into a very small room. I entered and found a small bookcase with several books and a small round table with a Bible lying on top. I looked in the bookcase and found several Sunday school books, a couple of daily devotionals, and a book of Bible stories. I stepped over to the Bible, opened it, and began to read: "The fear of the LORD is the beginning of knowledge" (Prov. 1:7).

Then I looked up and saw another door opening. I walked through and found another room, much larger than the first. I walked through carrying the open Bible with me. The room had several bookcases filled with many books. I saw reference books, Bible dictionaries, commentaries, study Bibles, books with maps, and much more.

I began to investigate these books when I saw another door open. I walked through with curiosity, still holding the open Bible in my hand. This room was huge! It was larger than any library I had ever seen. I was amazed at the many bookcases placed across the room filled with all sorts of books. There were books of famous Christian preachers and autobiographies of missionaries and their life's work for Christ. There were reference and commentary books, devotionals, and encouragement books of all kinds. I was almost giddy as I danced across the room from shelf to shelf to see the interesting books for me to read.

But as I reached for one, I saw another door opening. I held the Bible tight as I slowly walked toward this new door. In amazement, I walked through, stunned in total awe. I saw a room larger than any room I had ever seen or even heard about or seen in a magazine. Its walls and bookcases were endless; they seemed to go on for miles. I could not see the end of it. There were hundreds of bookshelves across the room with a limitless amount of books, parchments, and tablets of all sorts and languages. Then I looked up and realized that the ceiling seemed to reach to heaven, and there were staircases all around to reach hundreds more bookcases. Each level led up to another with more books, Bibles, music, and all things that pertained to my God and His Son, Jesus Christ.

I could hardly contain my excitement and joy at what I had seen. I was so awestruck that I closed my open Bible. Suddenly, I found myself back in the small room I started in, and I awoke.

This was God's way of showing me that He could teach me about Himself if I wanted to learn. He wanted me to know that He had an endless supply of knowledge, understanding, and wisdom to give me. He whispered in my ear, "Blessed are they that hunger and thirst after righteousness for they shall be filled" (Matt. 5:6). I finally understood that when I seek Him, I will find Him, and it will create a desire to know Him more. He is the only one who can satisfy my desire. He also revealed to me that learning about Jesus and my Father in heaven was an endless journey. Then I realized something profound. The rooms that kept getting bigger showed me that the more I learned, the less I really know, because there was still so much more to learn.

When I think I have become so knowledgeable about God, I realize I can always learn something new that I did not know. So I often tell people this story to illustrate a truth. If we will just begin to study God's Word, He will reveal Himself to us and lead us to more.

But the open Bible is the key. Unless we open God's Word, the other multitude of books and resources are meaningless. After all, the Bible is God's Word and His love letter to us. It is His road map and book of directions for our lives. We need it as much as we need water to drink and air to breathe. It is about the most important person in history, Jesus. He is our Savior, and He alone has the gift of eternal life for us and a home in heaven with our Father and Creator, God Almighty.

When you begin to read God's Word, you will find rooms of knowledge for yourself, and they will open to you year after year. The last room you will find is the most beautiful; it's heaven of course. I'll see you there.

2. A Conversation with Jesus— Intimacy through Prayer

ONE MORNING as I began my prayers, I heard Jesus calling me. My prayers had been short, and I had started my day without Him. However, it was Jesus who came to me as I heard Him whisper in my mind, "I know you heard me calling, so why do you stand so far off?"

I realized, in a moment, that my prayers were inadequate, impersonal, superficial, and distant, and that I hurried through them so I could get back to my activities. I bowed my head and said, "Lord, please forgive me; I know that I have placed many things ahead of You. You have done so much for me, and yet I have done little to love You in return."

Then the Lord said, "Come closer. I want you close to Me."

As I drew closer, I could feel His love glowing for me, and I began to repent of all the things that had kept me away from Him. That second cup of coffee, the news, the dishes, the laundry, the children, my work, and the list went on and on from morning until night. Then the Lord said, "Yes, I know about the things that keep you from Me. I watch you throughout the day, calling to you, and sometimes telling you things you should or should not do. Sometimes you seem to listen, but then you turn and go your own way. My heart is saddened that you will not let Me help you. Sadder yet that you don't love Me enough to stop and spend time with Me."

As I approached His throne, I knelt and asked Jesus to forgive me. Tears filled my eyes as I realized I had given my time to things that would pass away, even though I knew His love would never pass away. He was always available to encourage, strengthen, and love me through my day. I heard Him say, "Come up here, my child, and sit beside Me, and let us talk awhile."

I was humbled and honored by this request, so I moved closer. I looked up into His eyes as unworthiness swept over me, and I realized my sin. But He knew my thoughts, and He said tenderly. "I left the throne of glory, and counted it but loss; I bore the sin and suffering on the cruel cross. My child, do not be saddened, I did this all for you, so take my hand and follow close to me."[1]

My eyes filled with tears again as I took my place beside Him, and I bowed my head in reverence only to see a sight that broke my heart. I saw His nail-pierced hands. I slowly raised my head and again said, "My Lord, please forgive me; I am so sorry for the way I have treated You and neglected You. Please forgive me."

Jesus looked at me and smiled. "Don't you see, My child, I have forgiven you. You are forgiven, because I took your sin punishment. Your

---

[1] Ira Stanphill, "Follow Me," Singspiration, Hymn book, 1953.

debt is paid, and you are now free. You do not need to feel any guilt for your past, because I have removed it as far as the east is from the west, and I remember it no more" (Ps. 85:2; Matt. 9:2; Ps. 103:12).

I saw the joy in His face, and I knew that He had redeemed me for eternity to be His child. His love washed over me, and I began to smile and feel the peace that passes all understanding (Phil. 4:6).

Then Jesus said, "Now, my child, I have a request I want you to consider. I miss our time together, so please come to Me often, and let us sit and talk together. I love you and want to help you through your day to show you how you can serve Me best and contribute to My eternal plan for humankind."

"Oh yes, Lord, what a privilege. I would be glad to do that!"

Then the Lord said something I did not expect. "You will have to give up the world and its attraction. Do you remember when I said if you save your life, you will lose it, but if you lose your life for My sake, you will save it? This means I will be first in your life. When I call you, you will listen and obey. It means you will come to Me in the mornings to receive strength and direction for your day. You will live a life of love and peace and will joyfully share My message with others! You will talk to Me throughout your day, and I will encourage you, and you will know that I am always with you. I love you with an everlasting love, and I desire you to love Me in return. You are My ambassador for the kingdom, and I will empower you to be an able minister of reconciliation. My love will constrain you and give you victory. So sit here awhile, and let us share our love together. Then you will go out with a holy light on your face, and people will know that you have been with Me" (Rom. 12:2; Luke 9:24; Matt. 6:33; Ps. 5:3; Heb. 13:5b; Jer. 31:3; 2 Cor. 5:18–20; Exod. 34:30).

My answer was "Yes, Lord, I accept Your request, and through Your strength I will serve You all my days."

For Christian people everywhere, we must all, in silent prayer, confess our sins (1 John 1:9) and remember that we are redeemed and set free from an eternal death and given eternal life. I pray each person will make Christ Jesus first in their life

(Matt. 6:33) and love Him with their whole heart (Matt. 22:37). Give Him thanks and praise for renewing you today, and then arise with His victory shining on your face!

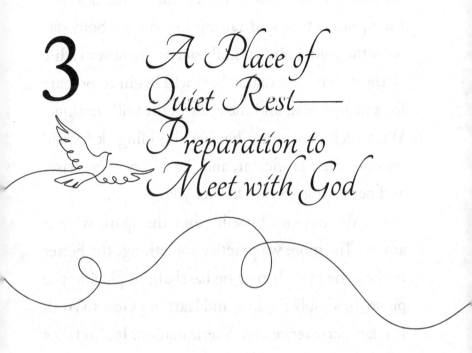

3 A Place of Quiet Rest— Preparation to Meet with God

THE SPARROW is a faithful and industrious little bird. Before she can lay her eggs, she must find a safe and secure place to make her nest. She diligently searches for twigs and straw to form the nest and then lines it with grass, leaves, and other materials to make it a soft and warm bed for her eggs. Then, with the preparations complete, she settles down to lay her eggs and wait for them to hatch. Soon another task begins as she diligently searches for food to feed them. She carefully watches over them, protecting and raising her young. Someday soon the young birds will fly out of the nest to a life of their own. The mama bird will begin to prepare for a new season, and the cycle of life will continue. With each generation her nest-building skills will become more proficient, and she will become wiser and better able to care for her young.

We too can benefit from the sparrow's example. The more we practice something, the better we become at it. It may be baseball, or playing the piano, or simply reading and learning God's Word. It takes persistence and determination. It also takes a listening ear and humble spirit. We will begin to develop an appetite for the Word as we read and study each day. Over time we will grow and become mature as we are changed and transformed into the image of God. That is the exciting part—to see the change and be excited at what God is doing in our lives! Of course this transformation does not happen overnight, and it takes preparation and a desire to learn and grow.

I am reminded of children when they look forward to the first day of a new school year. Their excitement is evident as they shop for new note-books, pencils, backpacks and clothes for the new year. Finally, with their backpack full of new treasures, they greet their friends with giggles and laughter.

We too should be excited and prepared as we meet with God each day. We look forward to our quiet time with God as we set aside a time each day and make ready our special place. We gather together our Bible, devotion books, journal, and various supplies we will need. Then we begin to quiet ourselves to meet with the God of the universe, our Savior and friend. We should begin with worship and praise and then move into a conversation with the Lord. In prayer we lay our concerns at the Savior's feet and slowly feel our burdens being lifted. Peace comes to our heart, and a smile will come to our face as we thank him for his unconditional love. We will always be encouraged as we read God's Word and find He brings clarity to our lives. You will hear him whisper in your ear, "This is the way, walk in it" (Isa. 30:21).

After a wonderful time of fellowship with the Lord is complete, say Amen. Then rise with renewed strength to begin your day. Turn to look back at this place of quiet rest, not to say goodbye but to say, "See you again tomorrow, Lord." Then hear Him reply, "I'll be waiting for you."

4 God's Workmanship and Masterpiece in a Time of Sorrow

ONE DAY, a sense of sadness came over me, and I felt empty. At that time, my church seemed to be disjointed, with no leadership, and its sheep seemed scattered. I longed to help and contribute my knowledge, but it was not welcomed. Frustration settled in on my heart and my mind. Then I prayed and asked God to take this burden away and give me peace. He showed me a story from *Streams in the Desert*,[2] August 19, about sorrow and joy. It lifted

---

[2] L. B. Cowman, *Streams in the Desert*, August 19 devotion, Zondervan, 1997.

my burden, and I learned to be "sorrowful, yet always rejoicing."

I knew that God knows everything; He sees tomorrow, and he holds it in His hand. These circumstances were no surprise or concern to Him because He knew the outcome. No matter what the situation, it is all within His eternal plan. Then this story came into my mind, and I knew it was a whisper from my heavenly Father.

The master sat at his loom working on his masterpiece, carefully placing each stitch. A little child passed by and curiously began to watch the master at work. The child looked at the master's face as he worked and saw his furrowed brow and the intent concentration on his work. He saw his face begin to change to a smile as his brow lifted and a twinkle was seen in his eyes. Then he heard a faint chuckle and a hum in his voice. As the child continued to watch the master, he noticed his expressions change from time to time. Like the rhythm of a song, his pace would go from slow and gentle to quick and intense. His work was steady, and he did not stop but made each stitch with love and care.

Then the child said, "I see you put great care

and commitment into your work, but all I see are knots and disjointed strings running from place to place with no rhyme or reason. I see no design in this work."

The master smiled at the child and said, "That's because you are looking from the world's perspective, and therefore, you cannot understand the reason for what you see. However, someday you will see it from my perspective, and you will under-stand why it must be done so."

After a while the child slipped over to the master's side and again looked upon the other side of the master's work. "Oh, how beautiful," remarked the child. "It is truly a work of art. I would have never imagined this design or the degree of your love that it took to create it. I am blessed to see it."

There will always be times in our lives when we do not understand our circumstances, so we must remember, "For now we see through a glass darkly, but then face to face: now I know in part; but then shall I know even as also I am known" (1 Cor. 13:12). Our lives may seem like the back of a tapestry, but we must trust the one who holds us in the palm of His hand and believe He is creating in us a work of beauty. We are His workmanship (Eph. 2:10)—His masterpiece. We must trust Him (Prov. 3:5–6).

5 Sharing the Treasures of Life—God's Gifts from Heaven

ALONG LIFE'S ROAD, I see that God has placed wonderful treasures for me to find. Sometimes these treasures are wonderful, but sometimes there are painful circumstances in my life. These treasures can be compared to beautiful jewels and come in various forms. At first glance these treasures do not appear beautiful. Most are disguised and appear plain and simple until the Lord shines on them with His love and unveils their beauty.

So as I journey through life, I cherish these treasures and hold them in my basket of remembrances. One stone of remembrance was the color of a ruby. That was the time I realized it was the color of the blood Christ shed for me. Another time I had a clear experience of God's forgiveness, and it glistened like a diamond as it changed my heart. Another time I learned some wonderful truths from God's Word, and they were like a string of pearls about my neck. Over many years I have found many treasures, and they have been blessings as if they had been silver and gold. God is always laying beautiful treasures along my path, and even though I don't recognize their beauty at the time, I collect them in my basket of remembrances.

Many times I stop to review all my treasures and find He has changed plain stones into beautiful jewels. I remember how He has changed me, too. So now, as I go along my way, God will impress me to share my treasures to encourage people in my path. I will share my stones of remembrance and show how God changed my rock of circumstance into a beautiful treasure of warmth and love. I often share how God's presence is always with me and how

He leads me down life's path. I explain how people's lives can shine like diamonds when they trust Christ as Savior and Lord.

And on and on it goes throughout my life. We will find treasures and then we must pass them on (Rom. 10:15, 17). The Lord often whispers to me and says, "Thank you for sharing My love with others. I left these treasures on the roadside of your life, and I am thankful you have learned to cherish them. Thank you for helping those in need and telling them how they can come to know Me as their personal savior. Thank you for receiving Me, loving Me, and sharing My love with others."

"… continue in my love …" (John 15:9)

6 *Wisdom—A Commentary*

ONCE UPON A TIME, the members of our Bible class got together to reorganize and move forward. Philippians 3:13–14 became our verse: "forgetting those things which are behind, and reaching forth to those things which are before, we press toward the mark for the high calling of God in Christ Jesus." With that in mind, we adopted a new name for our class—The Wisdom Seekers!

By studying God's Word, we "seek God's wisdom"! Wisdom is not hard to find; you simply need to study God's word, pray, and have a committed spirit to hear God's voice. The problem sometimes comes when we find it! God's wisdom is *sometimes* difficult for us to embrace. Let me explain.

Let's say you want to buy some new clothes. You look for the style you desire and after going to several stores, you finally find just what you want. The problem is that it is one size too small. This means that if you want to *fit* into that outfit, you must lose weight. That's a problem! Most of the time, we don't want to go on the diet that will lose the weight so we can *fit* into the clothes. However, if we are committed and diligent, we *do* lose the weight, and we are able to wear the clothes, and we look beautiful!

Let me further explain this parable. There are things in our lives that we need help with. We have decisions to make. So we seek wisdom and read God's Word. We also listen to preaching in church, on the radio, in devotions, and we pray. Several times we have seen the answer to our situation, but "embracing wisdom" is difficult. Sometimes it means we must give up something. Sometimes wisdom does not *fit* our desired outcome, and we must "lose weight," or spiritually speaking, we must sacrifice *our will*.

Gentle Whispers From My Heavenly Father

At one time or another, we have all prayed for wisdom. We know we need it, but it is the Holy Spirit of God who will show us how to get it. When we see God reveal wisdom to us, we find it is hard to apply it to our lives. We realize, in order for wisdom to be effective, we must *change*. However, we find we cannot change ourselves, and therefore must relinquish our will and allow the Holy Spirit to change us.

I believe that is just what God intends! He wants to conform us into His image! After all—*It is His wisdom!* We must let God mold and shape us so we can "put on wisdom" and model it to the world for all to see (Prov. 2:6; Eph. 4:24).

Wisdom comes in many shapes and sizes so it will *fit* everyone and all situations. I hope you will seek wisdom—and when you find it, I hope you will have the courage and the love for God to do whatever is necessary to "put it on" to reveal to the world "Christ in you" (Prov. 4:7; James 1:5).

7 *Where Is Your Samaria?*

I ONCE HEARD about the passing of Chuck Colson.[3] He was once on President Nixon's staff, but the corruption of Watergate was his downfall. Well, at least for a while. The time he spent in prison changed his life, and he would later say he was thankful for his time there. It was in prison he found and received Christ as his Savior and began

---

[3] Colson, Chuck; American lawyer, politician, public servant and Christian advocate. He was Nixon's chief counsel 1969–1973. He served seven months in prison related to the Watergate scandal.

to have a heart for people in prison. So when he was released, he began Prison Fellowship Ministry.[4]

As I thought on this, the Lord spoke to me about how most people don't know what God can do with their lives until they "hit bottom" and turn their lives over to Christ. I imagine that is what Chuck Colson did. He probably never dreamed that all his talents and abilities would be used for a worldwide ministry to prisoners. However, it is when we allow God to lead us that we discover our spiritual gifts. I imagine Chuck was amazed to find his time in prison led him to his "Jerusalem, Judea, Samaria, and the uttermost parts of the earth" (Acts 1:8). It was Jesus who told His disciples, "I must needs go through Samaria" (John 4:4).

So where is your Samaria? It may be way past where or what you could ever imagine (Eph. 3:20). In Matthew 28:19–20, Jesus calls Christians to "Go"! It is a command to seek and to save the lost and teach His word. In Acts 1:8 we are told to go, here and everywhere, to be His witnesses. God has equipped each of us with various talents, abilities,

---

[4] Prison Fellowship – Founded by Chuck Colson in 1976, to serve those incarcerated and to transform their lives in Christ.

and spiritual gifts, because there are countless needs in the world.

Some of us find ourselves drawn to nurse the sick, to teach, or to organize, and others to create and build. Some of us are satisfied to sit at a computer all day, but others need the fresh air of the outdoors. Wherever God calls you to go, you should *go!* (Col. 3:23). Of course, the *where* may surprise you, but God calls us to a variety of places. God may call you to serve in your hometown or a nearby city. Some are called far away, even to another country. However, there are times when God speaks to us, and we just don't listen. Sometimes we simply say *no*. We have that choice—God gave us a free will to choose.

Except saying *no* will not change your gifts or abilities or His call (Eph. 4:1). You may try to ignore God's calling, but eventually He will lead you to accept it. He will draw you by the power of His Holy Spirit and will put a passion within you—and you will *go* (Eph. 1:18a). You will never be truly happy until you say, "Yes, Lord," and submit to His will. When you submit, He will show you "your Samaria." It might take a while as He prepares you for your ultimate service, but all along the path there is a process of learning, growing, and following His way. You will hear His voice more clearly each day (2 Tim. 3:16–17).

Someday you will discover where God wants you to serve. So if you have yet to discover what calling God has for you, you can simply ask Him! Then submit to Him and wait on Him, and He will show you your place of calling—your Samaria. You were created for it.

8

The Traveling Man of Salvation

THERE WAS A MAN who went out from his company to sell his product. He thought highly of the product and believed in it. However, over many years he sold very few of them.

Each time he reported to his supervisor, he was asked, "Why haven't you sold the product?"

He would answer, "Well, I can't seem to find anyone who is interested."

His supervisor asked, "Do you tell them about your product? Do you demonstrate your product? I am sure if you did this, everyone would want it."

"Yes, it would seem so," he replied, "but I can't seem to find the right people to show it to. But I'll keep trying." The man would again leave and go back out into the marketplace, but alas, he would come back without any sales.

When pressed again by his supervisor, he would give vague answers and excuses of a lack of opportunities or abilities. There was always a reason for his failure to succeed.

Finally, his supervisor said he would go with him and see if he could determine the reason for his lack of sales. The man went through his day as usual with the supervisor watching from a distance. At the end of a week, the supervisor said, "Do you really believe in our product?"

"Oh yes" replied the man.

"Do you really believe that people need our product?" asked the supervisor.

"Oh yes," said the man.

"I have watched you," the supervisor said, "and it appears to me that you neither believe in the product, nor do you think people really need it."

The supervisor continued, "I see you talk to people. Sometimes you are friendly, and sometimes you're not, but you rarely talk about our product, and you very rarely demonstrate it. When you do talk about it, it is with someone who already has the product. You seem to talk about it quite a bit then. But to people who do not have our product, you do not even show it to them or talk about it. You make excuses to yourself and do not take advantage of the opportunity."

When they arrived back at the office, the supervisor turned to the salesman and said "I believe you know about our product and believe it is beneficial, but I don't believe you have ever tried our product for yourself—I mean you have never 'personally experienced it'!"

The salesman turned his head a bit and said, "Well, I thought I had. I know a lot about it."

"Yes," said the supervisor, "but you have never personally experienced it. You have never used it for yourself, and that's why you cannot sell it to others who really need it."

The supervisor told the salesman he would have to attend a training seminar on the product, where he would be asked to try out the product personally, and if he was unable to personally embrace the product, he would be terminated from the company. However, if he was truly and honestly able to receive it for himself, with joy, then he would become a sensational salesman for the company. The salesman agreed and attended the training.

In the training, there was a presentation of the product, with all its benefits and uses. The salesman understood all the information but was then asked this question: "Why do you need this product for yourself?" This was a curious question, and he had to think very hard about it. He thought everyone should have it, but when he had to apply it to himself, he realized he never had.

In fact he had never even opened it or even smelled its fragrance. He then realized he was a hypocrite and felt ashamed. He went up to the instructor and confessed his wrongdoing and asked to be forgiven and to have another chance. The instructor handed him the product and said, "Open and drink."

With tears in his eyes, the man drank, and with a surprised look, he said, "It's amazing. I feel alive for the first time in my life. I feel like a weight has been lifted and I can fly. I had no idea what this product could really do—but now I do. I have experienced it personally, and I am so excited about it! It will be easy to tell others about it now, because it has given me strength and new words to share with others. It is more wonderful than I ever knew; I can hardly believe it. No wonder I couldn't get people to try it—because I had never tried it myself. But now it will be easy, and it will be exciting!"

The salesman completed the training and received his certificate and could now return to his office. He thanked his supervisor profusely for helping him see the product clearly, and then went out and became one of the company's greatest salesmen.

Are you like this salesman? Do you know about the gift of eternal life that our Lord Jesus extends to everyone? Do you only know *a lot about it*, but have never really personally experienced it for yourself? Then, I invite you to "open and drink" from God's Word and find in John 3:16 that God offers you eternal life. When you read Romans 3:23, it tells us everyone needs it, and Romans 5:8 tells us that Christ died for us. We find we don't deserve it and can't earn it from Ephesians 2:8–9. We see in 2 Peter 3:9 that God wants everyone to have it. So if you realize you don't have salvation and eternal life from Jesus, *you can*. Romans 10:9–10 and 13 will tell you to ask and receive God's greatest gift of love. Then go out and tell someone!

Gentle Whispers From My Heavenly Father

9   *To Suffer as Christ*

I RECENTLY HAD A BIRTHDAY, and like all birthdays, I expected someone to wish me a "Happy Birthday." I did get a couple of nice cards from my husband and mother-in-law, with hugs and kisses early that morning. A good friend remembered me with a gift, and that was very nice. I expected some other friends to say "Happy Birthday" later that day, but it didn't happen. I had remembered their birthdays with calls and cards, but they had forgotten me. Then to make it worse, even my children forgot me. There were no phone calls, texts or cards.

I was quite disappointed and a bit sad. Then the Lord whispered in my ear—"It's okay, I know how you feel. I was forgotten many times. I was ridiculed by many and even thrown out of My own hometown (Luke 4:29a). Even My closest friends fell asleep when I really needed them most, and later they ran away and hid (Mark 14:37, 50). Yes, I know how you feel; but I have not forgotten you. I am here for you and will never leave or forsake you (Heb. 13:5b). I love you—Happy Birthday!"

I should remember when I am sad or disappointed that it is not suffering. I am thankful to be comforted by the words of my Savior and know "by his stripes we are healed" (Isaiah 53:5). The apostle Paul spoke of Christ's sufferings in Philippians 3:10: "That I may Know Him; and the power of his resurrection, and the fellowship of his sufferings, being made conformable unto his death."

I know that Christ suffered physically, emotionally, and spiritually, so I could have eternal life. So when I am sad, disappointed, or even persecuted, I must remember 2 Corinthians 4:8–10: "We are troubled on every side, yet not distressed; we are perplexed, but not in despair; Persecuted, but not forsaken; cast down, but not destroyed; Always bearing about in the body, the dying of the Lord Jesus, that the life also of Jesus might be made manifest in our body," and verse 17, "For our light affliction, which is but for a moment, works in us a far more exceeding and eternal weight of glory."

Yes, I was disappointed because someone did not tell me "Happy Birthday," but I got over it quickly when I remembered what Christ has done for me. I must remember and "count it all joy" (James 1:2).

10 The Yard Sale— Based on a True Story

NOT LONG AFTER MOM PASSED, we set ourselves to the task of going through her belongings. Some were sentimental to us, and we kept them, but most were set aside for a yard sale. As we began to go through Mom's room, we found that she was a real pack rat! We knew she liked to keep things, but we soon discovered that was an understatement. Packed neatly in every drawer, box, and cubbyhole were endless stacks of cards and keepsakes from many, many years back! There were an abundance of writing tablets, and several listed the cards she had sent and received. They also included the occasion, the person's name, and the date! Mom kept a record of everything, and she seem to collect an endless amount of memorabilia! Everything was precious to her, and she kept it all as if it were price-less treasures!

We found packages of needles and thread, buttons, calculators, ink pens, and more writing tablets. As our search continued, we found brand-new house slippers, still in the box, unused. We also found a variety of what might have been gifts that were never used and never opened! It was quite the adventure of discovering each treasure. We also found stacks of photos, from her childhood up to the present day. Those took us hours to look through, until we were exhausted and had to quit for the day.

As our search went on, we packed up clothes, shoes, and accessories. Of course there was a purse to match each outfit! In the purses, we found only a little money, but in *every* purse there was an as-sortment of emery boards, ink pens, breath mints, and handkerchiefs! It was very humorous. Mom was a precious lady, and going through her room and her belongings gave us the utmost respect for her. Every discovery proved her love and respect for her family and friends, and it spoke of her quiet and honorable life.

Finally the day arrived for the yard sale. The ad was in the paper, the signs were erected on every corner, and everything was organized and in its place. Yes, it felt good—until the crowds of people began to come in search of their treasure. They knew just what they wanted and how much they wanted to pay, and of course, they won out. The day was fast and furious, and we were glad to see it end. We sold many of the goods, but still a lot was left. So we packed up the remainder and donated it to a resale shop to benefit the needy. It was a long, tiring process, this yard sale, and we were thankful for the support we were given from several faithful friends. Without them we would not have made it to the end and accomplished our task.

As I rested that evening, I began to think about everything we had gone through. Then the Lord spoke to my heart. I recalled watching the people that came to the yard sale and how they were each seeking out a treasure that was special to them. They were happy when they found something and went away satisfied. But some, of course, found nothing, and they went away empty-handed.

I thought how similar that was to seeking the treasure Christ offers us. People hurry through life, thinking they know just what will make them happy, only to find many disappointments. They are searching for something to satisfy their soul, that empty place inside them that only Christ can fill. If they find the treasure Christ offers and embrace it, they will be satisfied and content. For the treasure that Christ offers is salvation, forgiveness, and peace of mind.

Another thing I realized about this yard sale was that their search would have been in vain had we not been willing to do the hard work necessary to provide them with these treasures. It was a sacrifice, but it yielded a reward for those who found a treasure and a peaceful heart for us.

For people of faith, it is Jesus Christ who did the hard work that paid the price so we could have the treasure of heaven. Christ could see beyond His sacrifice to see the people who needed His precious gift of eternal life. Christ knew it was the only way to reconcile humanity to a holy God, and He

Gentle Whispers From My Heavenly Father

was willing to make that supreme sacrifice that we might live. He could see beyond the pain and sorrow to see the treasure. It was His gift.

So through this yard sale I could see Christ, His love, and the people's need for a Savior. It was the only thing that would satisfy their emptiness. Still today, people continue to pass salvation by, not realizing its value. Jesus lived and died, but He rose again, just as He said, and as the prophets had foretold in the Old Testament. Yes, He arose and is living today. He sits at the right hand of the Father, interceding for His children, and waiting for that day when He will return for His Church.

Are you searching today for some great treasure that will satisfy your longing? Look no more, my friend, for Christ has provided the greatest treasure of all time—eternal life. You can receive it by simply confessing your sin and asking the Savior, Jesus, for forgiveness. The price is paid, and the door is open. The Bible tells us in Matthew 7:7, "Ask and it shall be given, seek and you will find, knock and it shall be open unto you." Romans 10:9–10 tells you to "confess with your mouth the Lord Jesus and believe in your heart that God has raised him from the dead, and thou shalt be saved." But it is verse 13 that gives us assurance: "For whosoever shall call upon the name of the Lord *shall be* saved."

If you have found this treasure for yourself, please share it with others. It is a precious treasure—the gift of eternal life—and everyone needs it.

11 Slow Down so You Can See the Trees—A Fictional Story

WHEN I WAS A BOY, I took a train trip with my father. It was all very exciting and wonderful for a young boy, but the thing that I remember most are the trees. At first the train was going very slow, and I could see the landscape. It was autumn in New Hampshire, and the trees were a multitude of colors. Brilliant yellows, gorgeous reds and crimsons, bright orange, all mixed with the dark green fir trees and the mellow green of the pines. Together they were a beautiful sight. It was a wonder to behold. A portrait of God's glorious creation, and I looked in awe.

Soon the train began to pick up speed, and before I knew it, we were going very fast. Everything was speeding past me so fast that the landscape of trees began to blend together. No longer could I see each color, but it was as if they were all mixed together, and a new and different color emerged. I could not distinguish them individually, as they were all a blur, and I grew dizzy looking at them. I had to sit back in my seat to regain my focus.

Soon we reached our destination. It was my grandfather's farm. He had become ill, and my father told me he did not have many days left to live. So I was surprised to find Grandpa dressed and standing at the front door waiting for us. He greeted us warmly and gave us hugs that I thought were held much too long, but I didn't say anything. I watched Grandpa approach my dad. At first he just looked at him as tears welled up in his eyes, and then he gave him a hug that lasted a very long time.

There was silence for a bit, and then Grandpa said, "Well, come in, come in. I have some hot chocolate on the stove; you must be frozen." The sweet drink soon warmed us up, and the conversation began to be more lively. Grandpa asked me to bring in some more firewood from outside, and he said that later we would feed the stock together.

Later that day, I told my dad that Grandpa didn't look sick. He told me he was very ill and probably had only a few months to live. I felt very sad, because Grandpa was so nice and kind to me. My dad said, "He wasn't always nice and kind. This illness has humbled him greatly." I didn't understand, but I didn't ask any questions either because of the broken tone in my father's voice and the sad look on his face.

The afternoon passed quickly with chores, and we enjoyed a nice supper. Soon we were snug in our beds under tons of quilts and feather pillows. It was a nice feeling, and I slept like a rock.

Early the next morning, I woke to the smell of bacon frying and coffee perking on the stove. I quickly jumped out of bed and dressed warmly for the day. I ran downstairs to find my father and Grandpa sitting at the table having their coffee. "You're just in time, my boy," said Grandpa. "The biscuits just came out of the oven." The biscuits were as big as my fist, and they were hot and delicious with fresh butter and jelly. After breakfast, Grandpa asked me how I liked the train ride. I told him all about the trees and how at first I could see each one in its beauty, but as the train went faster, they all became a blur of colors. They were all mixed together and it made me dizzy.

Grandpa paused for a moment and just looked out across the room and seemed lost in his thoughts. "Are you okay, Grandpa"? I asked.

Slowly he answered, "Yes, I am fine. You just reminded me of my life."

"Really?" I said. "How did I do that?" He told me it was a long story, and that he would tell me all about it if I would take a long walk with him.

We bundled up warmly and began to walk out around the farm. "See those trees over there?" he asked.

"Sure, I see them," I replied.

"Well, tell me what you see."

The farm was behind us now, and a large forest lay ahead. I looked all around to my left and right, and then I said, "It's like when I was first on the train, and it was going slow. I could see all the trees and their colors, like now. I see so many different colors, and they are all beautiful."

Grandpa replied, "That's right, son, when you look at them individually, you can see the unique beauty of each one, and when you look at them all together, they make a beautiful sight to behold.

"It's a lot like life, you know. As we grow up we get tired of the same old things, and we want something new, something exciting, and when we look for it—well, it's a little like when you were on the train, and it began to go fast, and all the trees and their beauty just became a blur."

Grandpa paused and then continued, "Son, when I was about middle age, I began to care more about the busyness of life than I did about my family. I spent too much time chasing dreams than living in reality. My life was speeding by like that train, and all the real beauty in my life was just a blur to me. It wasn't until I got sick and I had to slow down that I realized what a mistake I had made. That is why I brought you out here to the trees so I could teach you a lesson. Look at those trees, and tell me what you see."

I took a long look and turned back to my grandpa and said, "Well, I see all kinds of different trees, Grandpa, and they all have different colors. They are all real pretty, too."

Grandpa laughed a little and said, "Yes, that's what most people would see. But let's look a little closer and see if we can find some buried treasures."

I laughed too and said, "Grandpa, buried treasure is for pirate ships, not the forest."

"Well, then," Grandpa said, "let's see if we can find some. See that big old oak over there? Look right near the top, and tell me what you see."

I looked hard and then was amazed. "It's an eagle! Grandpa, it's an eagle! Wow," I said with total amazement.

Then Grandpa said, "Now look over there in that grove of hardwoods, and tell me how many animals you see." I began to look, and at first I only saw a squirrel. Then after a few moments, I saw another squirrel and then a cardinal and some other birds. Grandpa said, "Look lower, at the ground." Another hard look revealed a surprise.

"It's a deer, Grandpa. I can hardly believe it."

 Gentle Whispers From My Heavenly Father

He replied, "Oh, you would be surprised what you might find if you would only look."

As we walked through the woods that day, we found rabbits, chipmunks, and a variety of birds, including an owl and two hawks. We saw the nests of birds and the burrows of small animals. Actually, I saw a whole village of wildlife. It was amazing to see how they all lived together. It was an experience I will never forget, but the lesson my grandpa taught me was the one that would change my life.

Grandpa had shut out most of the family that had loved him because he was going through life too fast, chasing his dreams. It took his illness to slow him down and bring him to see just what he had lost in his pursuit. Walking through the woods that day had shown me it takes time to see all there is to see, and you must take your time and look deep into each thing to finds its beauty and its treasure.

There is an old phrase that says, "You can't see the forest for the trees," which means that you are too close to something to see the whole picture. There is good merit in that, but I have found that in this story, it is more important to see each "tree" clearly so you can be part of the "forest." This means you need to look at each person closely and find the hidden treasure they hold. When you step back, you can see all the people or the "forest." It is then you see that God has really outdone Himself, for your family has beauty and value to enrich your life with many blessings. Your family is your forest, so treasure each and every one (Matthew 6:21),

Gentle Whispers From My Heavenly Father

12 Proud to Be among the Ranks

ARE YOU A SOLDIER FOR CHRIST? If you are a Christian, a follower of Christ, a believer in Jesus Christ, then you *should* be a soldier for Christ. What does that mean anyway? It means that we stand for what Christ Jesus stands for. He is God, Savior, Redeemer, Lord, and soon coming King. What He stands for is clearly written in God's Word, the Bible. Have you read it?

I began to think of these things when I heard

a message by Adrian Rogers,[5] talking about raising our children. He encouraged parents to pay attention to their children and to actively participate in their everyday lives. You see, if we as parents go to church, read our Bibles, and live a life for Christ, then it will be our daily example that will influence our children. Not to just learn a routine or habit, but to learn to embrace a love for Christ that comes from the heart.

Adrian Rogers spoke of a famous baseball player who credited his success to his Lord and Savior, Jesus Christ. He spoke of how important his family was to him. Even though he was chosen to be in the Baseball Hall of Fame, his desire was to someday be found in God's Hall of Fame. His desire was to be an example of Christ, and so his love for Christ constrained him to spend time with his family and live his faith in front of them. I believe that his example proved to be successful in that his family became devoted followers of Christ.

As an individual Christian, each of us looks at our life and thinks that we are nothing special.

---

[5] Adrian Rogers, pastor of Bellevue Baptist Church in Memphis, Tennessee, from 1972 to 2005.

 Gentle Whispers From My Heavenly Father

Aside from being an outstanding ballplayer, this man was not any different from most Christians. We struggle with many things, and we have our share of trials. We go to church, pray, read our Bibles, and participate in the activities at church and our community. But there is only one thing that sets apart those who might be found in God's Hall of Fame. That one thing is love and a heart's desire to serve our risen Lord. It is our passion to keep on keeping on every day. As 2 Corinthians 4:8–10 says, "We are troubled on every side, yet not distressed, we are perplexed, but not in despair; Persecuted, but not forsaken; cast down, but not destroyed; Always bearing about in the body the dying of the Lord Jesus, that the life also of Jesus might be made known in our lives."

Our "pressing towards the mark" (Phil. 3:14) is a daily process, and it is only with God's help through the Holy Spirit that we can be successful. For it is not by any works that we have done that we attain salvation and heaven (Eph. 2:8–9). It is only because of the blood of Jesus. However, we are able to carry on each day because of the strength He gives us, and our hope is in Him. So we put one foot in front of the other each morning, quoting Ephesians 6:10–18. We put on the armor of God because we are warriors for Christ, and it is a battle out there. We stand shoulder to shoulder with other Christians around the world, even though it seems like we are alone in the fight.

However, we are not alone. Christ is with us, and we stand with many Christians, holding forth our shield of faith in a wicked world. We are victors in Christ. We win—never forget that! We are forging a path for the next generation, just like the prophets, apostles, and early Christians did before us. We must remember that we are soldiers of the cross. We are making a difference.

When I look across a grassy meadow and see its lush carpet of green, I am reminded of the vastness of the world. However, when I look closer, I see thousands of wildflowers and tiny living creatures thriving within each blade of grass. The body of Christ is like that: we are still thriving in the world, sometimes unseen, but standing firm for Christ.

You may not ever be in the World's Hall of Fame, but you can be in God's Hall of Fame. Be proud to be among the ranks and privileged to serve a risen Savior. One day we will hear, "Well done thy good and faithful servant ... enter into the joys of the Lord" (Matt. 25:23). Amen.

13 Going Home Again

YOU MAY HAVE HEARD it said, "You can't go home again." This phrase really refers to the way things used to be or the way you remember home. The meaning behind this phrase is true; however, accepting its truth may actually enable you to go home again.

Many of us graduated from high school and went off to college and then pursued a career that took us away from home. Some got married and moved away, and some entered into military service and were changed forever. Then there were some who just wanted to get away and get out on their own. In any case, something took us far away from home. In those early years we were very excited to get away from home, but as the years passed, some of us wished we had never left home and wanted to go home again.

But you can't really "go home" again. That's because time changes things. It changes the people you grew up with and the towns you lived in. Towns grow larger and undergo urban sprawl, and when you do get home for a visit, you can't even find your way around. You are usually astounded by the commercial growth and the disappearance of the fields and woods you once played in. Gone is the cow pasture you played ball in; but thankfully, it has been replaced with a new ballpark, complete with four fields, parking, and restrooms. You take a nostalgic drive past your old high school only to find it gone. It was torn down, and a field of grass remains.

Yes, things change. People change too. Like you, they grew up. Not only have they lost their hair and gained weight, wrinkles, and grandchildren, but their goals, attitudes, and beliefs have changed, some for the worse. Some have passed away, but others have attained success in ways that surprise you.

Our fond memories of our hometown and our friends and family are just that—memories. They are wonderful and cherished, but they are a time gone by. Sweet memories are forever locked in our hearts and minds. No, we can't go back to those childhood days, for they are long since gone and have taken some of ourselves with it. The desire to "go home again" is in large part based on those wonderful memories, and that's why you can't "go home again." That time does not exist anymore. It is a sweet memory and not the reality of the here and now. However, knowing and accepting the reality of change will free you to be able to go home again.

Many of us long to return to our hometown after being away for many years. In fact, you may have thought often of moving back to your hometown, but personal situations, commitments, and your life choices prevented you from going. For some, the thought of moving home becomes a dream that may never come true. Of course we do manage to go home for a visit from time to time to see family but not to live there. However, for some, going home can be a reality—almost a dream come true. But remember who you are. You are older now and not the same person you were growing up. Get ready for a change.

Going home at this time of your life is like moving to a new town with new people while making a new life for yourself. Oh, you may renew old friendships, but it won't be the same, because you are not the same. It is a time for new beginnings and new experiences—making a new home. Yes, it will be a joy to live near family members dear to your heart. After all, that's probably the real reason you wanted to go home.

Now, there will be wonderful new memories waiting to be made. There may possibly be new jobs and for sure new friendships and new challenges. It will be an exciting time and very rewarding. Just keep in mind, it's not that home of yesteryear you remember. It's something better: it's home, filled with love and hope of a new tomorrow.

In a similar way, there may have been a time in your life when you accepted Christ as your Savior (John 3:16). As we see in the example above, time and life change us. Many times in our lives, our jobs and our personal pursuits take us away from our devotion to Christ. We stop going to church and reading the Bible, and our thoughts are on worldly things and not heavenly things. Then there usually comes a crisis in our lives, and we begin to call out to the Lord for help. It is then we realize just how far we have drifted away from our faith and our God.

Much like the Prodigal Son (Luke 15:11–24), we realize the error of our ways and determine to make things right. So we return to church and to the Lord and have a new peace in our hearts. It is like "going home" again. Yes, going home is a wonderful thing—whether it's to your hometown or to the Lord.

14 *A Life Lived—A Fictional Story*

IT HAD BEEN A HORRIBLE DAY at work, and I brought my anger and frustrations home and spilled them on my wife and children. Now, with hurt feelings all around, we each retreated to our rooms—except I found myself in the guest room and without supper. I was exhausted and I fell across the bed muttering how this was all God's fault. Soon I was asleep, and I began to dream.

I dreamed that God the Father pulled back the curtain of heaven and said, "See this man? I sent this child into the world. He was a bright lad, went to school, and learned many things. He went to college, graduated with high honors, and received a degree. He fell in love and got married and raised a family. He ran a successful business and made plenty of money. He bought many things and enjoyed the pleasures of life in this world. He later retired well, but he soon died."

Then the Lord said to me, "This man came and stood before me and wanted to come into heaven, but I would not let him pass. The man said, 'I've done well in the world, and accomplished many things. Why will you not let me enter heaven?' And I said, 'You have not done well. I do not know you—you are not my child'" (Matthew 7:23).

The Lord continued, "I gave you instructions and direction for your life, but you did not follow them. I made Myself available to you, but you never called on Me. I sent people to intervene in your life when you were in trouble, but you refused their help. You have broken My heart with your rejection. You have done things your way all your life. You did not want My help. Now you come to the end of your life, and you find you have no eternal life. I do not know you because you did not call Me a father, and

 Gentle Whispers From My Heavenly Father

you did not receive My salvation through My Son, Jesus Christ. Depart from me; I never knew you."

I awoke from the dream with tears in my eyes, for I knew I was the man the Lord was talking about. As I slid down onto my knees, I called out to God with a repentant and broken heart. "O God, forgive me for rejecting You, and forgive me of my sin of unbelief. You are right that I have only lived for myself, and I now ask for Your forgiveness. I accept Your gift of eternal life through Jesus Christ and declare Him this day to be the Lord of my life" (Romans 6:23, 10:13).

"Oh, thank You, dear Father, that in Your mercy You have pulled back the curtain of time to show me my life and what might have been. Let me now embrace You and Your Word and heed its instruction that I might live a life that is well pleasing to the Father."

As I ended my prayer and wiped the tears from my eyes, I stood up to see a beautiful sight. Standing in the doorway were my wife and my children. With tears they ran to embrace me. As we held on to each other, I began to explain, "You see, I had this dream—"

But my wife interrupted and said, "There is no need to explain, for you see your dream was an answer to my prayer—a prayer to unite our family as one, under God. Thank You, heavenly Father, for answered prayer" (James 5:16b). And we all said, "Amen."

15 Faith in Christ— or Something Else?

THE BIBLE TELLS US in Hebrews 11:6, "Without faith it is impossible to please him: for he that comes to God must believe that he is, and that he is a rewarder of them that diligently seek him."

Do you have faith, and if you do, does it please God? What kind of faith do you have? I hear about many people today who talk about their "healing faith." They search everywhere and do many things to be healed of their ailments. Their "faith for healing" is not really faith, but it is an act of desperation to find relief from their pain or ailment. They may have heard of someone or something that promises healing, so they seek it out. They usually seek a person who claims they can "heal" their infirmity, but they are usually disappointed.

Sickness and pain can bring depression, and it is most unkind to our bodies. It can be devastating and debilitating and bring the fear of death. People seek to be healed and restored to health, so they seek whatever it takes to be whole again. We go to doctors, take medications, and endure treatments, even surgeries. Some are justified and do bring healing, but some do not. Most often our "faith" is in a person, treatment, or medicine and not in our God.

I believe it is only the God of heaven who can bring healing. I believe God can and does heal, but He does not always bring a physical healing. People who have placed their faith in the Lord Jesus Christ as their Savior know how He brings healing. He can and does bring emotional and spiritual healing of our souls. One day those who believe in the Lord Jesus Christ will be eternally healed at His return. It is then that we will experience a "physical" healing, when our temporary bodies are transformed into an immortal, incorruptible and glorified body at His

Gentle Whispers From My Heavenly Father

coming (1 Thess. 4:16–17; 1 Cor. 15:51–53)! Praise God, we look forward to this wonderful event.

But until then, we must live every day by faith. That includes our physical bodies. There are days that I have experienced physical pain, and I have prayed God would touch me and relieve the pain. Some days my pain is relieved, and some days it is not, but I know God loves me and knows about my pain. I must have faith to trust Him. When I focus on God's Word, I know He will sustain me, and I feel His presence. It is then I am comforted. When I remember the suffering Christ endured on the cross as He paid the penalty for my sin, my pain doesn't seem as bad. It is a matter of perspective.

I am not minimizing our pain, for truly many people do live with a great deal of pain and discomfort. I am thankful that we have doctors and medicine to relieve our pain and treatments that sometimes cure our pain. God has given knowledge and wisdom to physicians to promote healing, and we should take advantage of their help. But ultimately, we need to depend on the Lord Jesus and ask Him to comfort, heal, and direct us.

I remember the story of Peter walking on the

water. He had a little faith to step out of the boat and begin to walk on the water toward Jesus, but when he saw the wind and the waves, he began to look at the storm and not at Christ, and he began to sink. In his cry of distress, Peter called out for Jesus to save him: "And immediately Jesus stretched forth his hand, and caught him, and said O thou of little faith, wherefore did thou doubt?" (Matt. 14:31).

Our focus needs to be on Jesus Christ, our Savior, Lord, Redeemer, and soon coming King! It is Jesus who watches over us every hour of the day and can intervene at any moment in our distress. It is the ever-present power of the Holy Spirit within us that can bring peace into our hearts and minds, because we trust in Christ (Phil. 4:6–7). It is that faith that will see us through whatever comes our way.

I am reminded of the story about the ten lepers in Luke 17:11–19. Can you imagine having this debilitating and horrible disease? It slowly eats away at your flesh and makes you an outcast among your own family and community! These men lived sad and depressing lives, were forced to beg for their food, and had no one to care for them.

Gentle Whispers From My Heavenly Father

But then there was Jesus. They heard of Him healing others, and they wanted healing of their leprosy. They came asking for mercy. Jesus commanded them to show themselves to the priest, and "as they went, they were healed." But only one, when he saw he was healed, turned back and glorified God with thanksgiving. This man's faith was in the right place—in Jesus.

So many people today have misplaced faith. They have faith in everything except Jesus. Yes, Jesus still heals today, but not everyone is healed. God's Word tells us in Isaiah 55:8–9, "My thoughts are not your thoughts, neither are your ways my ways, saith the LORD. For as the heavens are higher than the earth, so are my ways higher than your ways, and my thoughts than your thoughts."

Our faith must stay strong whether we are healed or not. Christ Jesus can sustain you through His Word, and sometimes He uses friends. James 5:16 tells us to "confess your faults [or troubles] to one another and pray one for another, that ye may be healed. The effectual fervent prayer of a righteous man avails much." Yes, God places godly people in our path to encourage and pray for us. Going to a

Bible-believing church is always helpful, as you can hear God's Word preached and find a support system of caring friends.

I encourage you to trust in the Lord. It is through our faith in Christ and His Word that He brings comfort, peace, and assurance in every situation. For that kind of faith I say, "Thank You, Lord, and I give You praise as I worship You and You alone!"

Jesus said, "I will never leave or forsake you" (Hebrews 13:5b). This is a true statement and promise. He can encourage us, comfort us, sustain us, heal us, and carry us through anything in our lives. He is our hope of eternal life.

My hope is in Christ, and someday I will see Him face to face (1 Cor. 13:12). Until then, I live by faith.

Footnotes and Scripture References (KJV)

God's Rooms of Knowledge and Wisdom

Ps. 1:7   "the fear of the Lord is the beginning of knowledge."

Matt. 5:6   "Blessed are they that hunger and thirst after righteousness for they shall be filled."

A Conversation with Jesus – Intimacy through Prayer

1. Ira Stanphill, "Follow Me," Singspiration, Hymn book, 1953.

Ps. 85:2   "Thou hast forgiven the iniquity of thy people, thou hast covered all their sin."

Matt. 9:2   "And, behold, they brought to him a man sick of the palsy, lying on a bed: and Jesus seeing their faith said unto the sick of the palsy: Son, be of good cheer; thy sins be forgiven thee."

Ps. 103:12   "As far as the east is from the west, so far hath he removed our transgression from us."

Rom. 12:2	"And be not conformed to this world: but be ye transformed by the renewing of your mind, that ye may prove what is that good, and acceptable, and perfect, will of God."
Luke 9:24	"For whosoever will save his life shall lose it: but whosoever will lose his life for my sake, the same shall save it."
Matt. 6:33	"But seek ye first the kingdom of God, and his righteousness; and all these things shall be added unto you."
Ps. 5:3	"My voice shalt thou hear in the morning, O Lord; in the morning will I direct my prayer unto thee, and will look up."
Heb. 13:5b	"I will never leave thee, nor forsake thee."
Jer. 31:3	"The Lord hath appeared of old unto me, saying, Yea, I have loved thee with an everlasting love: therefore with lovingkindness have I drawn thee."
2 Cor. 5:18–20	"And all things are of God, who hath reconciled us to himself by Jesus Christ, and hath given to us the ministry of reconciliation;"
Ex. 34:29–30	"And it came to pass, when Moses came down from mount Sinai with the two tables of testimony in Moses' hand, when he came down from the mount, that Moses wist not that the skin of his

face shone while he talked with him. And when Aaron and all the children of Israel saw Moses, behold, the skin of his face shone."

1 John 1:9   "If we confess our sins, he is faithful and just to forgive us our sins, and to cleanse us from all unrighteousness."

Matt. 22:37   "Jesus said unto him, Thou shalt love the Lord thy God with all thy heart, and with all thy soul, and with all thy mind."

A Place of Quiet Rest - Preparation to Meet with God
Isa. 30:21   "This is the way, walk in it."

God's Workmanship and Masterpiece in a Time of Sorrow
2. L. B. Cowman, Streams in the Desert, August 19 devotion, Zondervan, 1997.

1 Cor. 13:12   "For now we see through a glass darkly, but then face to face: now I know in part; but then shall I know even as also I am known."

Eph. 2:10   "For we are his workmanship, created in Christ Jesus unto good works, which God hath before ordained that we should walk in them."

Prov. 3:5–6   "Trust in the Lord with all your heart and lean not unto your own understanding, and in all your ways acknowledge Him and He will direct your path."

Sharing the Treasures of Life—God's Gifts from Heaven

Rom. 10:15, 17   "And how shall they preach, except they be sent as it is written, How beautiful are the feet of them that preach the gospel of peace, and bring glad tidings of good things! ... So then faith cometh by hearing, and hearing by the word of God."

John 15:9   "Continue in my love."

Wisdom – A Commentary

Phil. 3:13–14   "Brethren, I count not myself to have apprehended: but this one thing I do, forgetting those things which are behind, and reaching forth to those things which are before, I press toward the mark for the prize of the high calling of God in Christ Jesus."

Rom. 8:29   "For whom he did foreknow, he also did predestinate to be conformed to the image of his Son, that he might be the firstborn among many brethren."

Eph. 4:24   "And that ye put on the new man, which after God is created in righteousness and true holiness."

Prov. 4:7	"Wisdom is the principal thing; therefore get wisdom: and with all thy getting get understanding."
James 1:5	"If any of you lack wisdom, let him ask of God, and giveth to all men liberally, and upbraided not: and it shall be given him."

Where Is Your Samaria?

3. Chuck Colson, American lawyer, politician, public servant and Christian advocate. He was Nixon's chief counsel 1969–1973. He served seven months in prison related to the Watergate scandal.

4. Prison Fellowship – Founded by Chuck Colson in 1976, to serve those incarcerated and to transform their lives in Christ.

Acts 1:8	"But ye shall receive power, after that the Holy Ghost is come upon you: and ye shall be witnesses unto me both in Jerusalem, and in all Judaea, and in Samaria, and unto the uttermost part of the earth."
John 4:4	"And he must needs go through Samaria."
2 Tim. 3:16–17	"All scripture is given by inspiration of God, and is profitable for doctrine, for reproof, for correction, for instruction in righteousness. That the man of God may be perfect [complete], thoroughly

	furnished [equipped] unto all good works."
Matt. 28:19–20	"Go ye therefore, and teach all nations, baptizing them in the name of the Father, and of the Son, and of the Holy Ghost: Teaching them to observe all things whatsoever I have commanded you: and, lo, I am with you always, even unto the end of the world. Amen."
Col. 3:23	"And whatsoever ye do, do it heartily as to the Lord, and not unto men;"
Eph. 1:4	"According as he hath chosen us in him before the foundation of the world, that we should be holy and without blame before him in love;"
Ephesians 1:8a	"The eyes of your understanding being enlightened; that ye may know what is the hope of his calling."

The Traveling Man of Salvation

John 3:16	"For God so loved the world, that he gave his only begotten Son, that whosoever believeth in him should not perish, but have everlasting life."
Rom. 3:23	"For all have sinned, and come short of the glory of God;"
Rom. 5:8	"But God commended his love toward us, in that, while we were yet sinners, Christ died for us."

Eph. 2:8–9	"For by grace are ye saved through faith; and that not of yourselves; it is the gift of God; Not of works, lest any man should boast."
2 Pet. 3:9	"The Lord is not slack concerning his promise ... not willing that any should perish, but that all should come to repentance."
Rom. 10:9–10	"That if thou shalt confess with thy mouth the Lord Jesus, and shalt believe in thine heart that God hath raised him from the dead, thou shalt be saved. For with the heart man believeth unto righteousness; and with the mouth confession is made unto salvation."
Rom. 10:13	"For whosoever shall call upon the name of the Lord shall be saved."

To Suffer as Christ

Luke 4:29a	"And rose up, and thrust him out of the city ..."
Mark 14:37, 50	"And he cometh, and findeth them sleeping, and saith unto Peter, Simon, sleepest thou? Could you not watch one hour? ... And they all forsook him, and fled."
Heb. 13:5b -	"I will never leave thee, nor forsake thee."
Isa. 53:5	"By his stripes we are healed."

Phil. 3:10	"That I may Know Him; and the power of his resurrection, and the fellowship of his sufferings, being made conformable unto his death."
2 Cor. 4:8–10, 17	"We are troubled on every side, yet not distressed; we are perplexed, but not in despair; Persecuted, but not forsaken; cast down, but not destroyed; Always bearing about in the body, the dying of the Lord Jesus, that the life also of Jesus might be made manifest in our body. ... For our light affliction, which is but for a moment, works in us a far more exceeding and eternal weight of glory."
James 1:2	"My brethren, count it all joy when ye fall into divers temptations."

The Yard Sale

Matt. 7:7	"Ask and it shall be given, seek and you will find, knock and it shall be open unto you."
Rom. 10:9–10	"That if thou shalt confess with your mouth the Lord Jesus, and believe in thine heart that God has raised him from the dead, and thou shalt be saved. For with the heart man believeth unto righteousness; and with the mouth confession is made unto salvation."

Rom. 10:13   "For whosoever shall call upon the
                      name of the Lord shall be saved."

Slow Down so You Can See the Trees
Matt. 6:21   "For where your heart is there will your
                      treasure be also."

Proud to Be among the Ranks
5. Adrian Rogers, pastor of Bellevue Baptist Church in
        Memphis, Tennessee, from 1972 to
        2005.

2 Cor. 4:8-10   "We are troubled on every side, yet not
                      distressed, we are perplexed, but
                      not in despair; Persecuted, but not for-
                      saken; cast down, but not destroyed;
                      Always bearing about in the body the
                      dying of the Lord Jesus, that the life
                      also of Jesus might be made known in
                      our lives."

Phil. 3:14   "I press toward the mark for the prize
                      of the high calling of God in Christ
                      Jesus."

Eph. 2:8–9   "For by grace are ye saved through
                      faith; and that not of yourselves: it is
                      the gift of God: Not of works, lest any
                      man should boast."

Eph. 6:10–18   "Finally, my brethren, be strong in the
                      Lord, and in the power of his might.
                      Put on the whole armor of God, that ye
                      may be able to stand against the wiles

of the devil. For we wrestle not against flesh and blood, but against principalities, against powers, against the rulers of the darkness of this world, against spiritual wickedness in high places. Wherefore take unto you the whole armor of God, that ye may be able to withstand in the evil day, and having done all, to stand. Stand therefore, having your loins girt about with truth, and having the breastplate of righteousness; and your feet shod with the preparation of the gospel of peace; above all, taking the shield of faith, wherewith ye shall be able to quench all the fiery darts of the wicked. And take the helmet of salvation, and the sword of the Spirit, which is the word of God; Praying always with all prayer and supplication in the Spirit, and watching thereunto with all perseverance and supplication for all saints."

Matt. 25:23

"His Lord said unto him, well done thy good and faithful servant, thou hast been faithful over a few things, I will make thee ruler over many things: enter into the   joys of the Lord."

Going Home Again

John 3:16

"For God so loved the world he gave his only begotten Son that whosoever believeth in him should not perish but have everlasting life."

| Luke 15:11–24 | "And the younger of them said to his father, Father, give me the portion of goods that fall to me ... and when he had spent all ... he began to be in want ... and when he came to himself ... I will arise and go to my father ... and say I have sinned ... when he was yet a great way off, his father saw him, had compassion on him ... kissed him ... put the best robe on him, a ring on his hand and shoes on his feet ... And they began to be merry." |

A Life Lived

Matt. 7:23	"And then will I profess unto them, I never knew you: depart from me, ye that work iniquity.
Rom. 6:23	"For the wages of sin is death; but the gift of God is eternal life through Jesus Christ our Lord.
Rom. 10:13	"For whosoever shall call upon the name of the Lord shall be saved."
James 5:16b	"The effectual fervent prayer of a righteous man avails much."

Faith in Christ—or something else?

| Heb. 11:6 | "But without faith it is impossible to please him: for he that comes to God |

must believe that he is, and that he is a rewarder of them that diligently seek him.

1 Thess. 4:16–17 "For the Lord himself shall descend from heaven with a shout, with the voice of the archangel, and with the trump of God: and the dead in Christ shall rise first; Then we which are alive and remain shall be caught up together with them in the clouds, to meet the Lord in the air; and so shall we ever be with the Lord."

1 Cor. 15:51–53 "Behold, I shew you a mystery; We shall not all sleep, but we shall all be changed, In a moment, in the twinkling of an eye; at the last trump: for the trumpet shall sound, and the dead shall be raised incorruptible, and we shall be changed. For this corruptible must put on incorruption, and this mortal must put on immortality."

Matt. 14:31 "And immediately Jesus stretched forth his hand, and caught him, and said O thou of little faith, wherefore did thou doubt?" (full story: Matt. 14:22–33)

Phil. 4:6-7 "Be careful for nothing; but in everything by prayer and supplication with thanksgiving let your requests be made known unto God. And the peace of God, which passeth all understanding, shall keep your hearts and minds through Christ Jesus."

Luke 17:13–14	"And they lifted up their voices, and said, Jesus, Master, have mercy on us. And when he saw them, he said unto them, Go show yourselves unto the Priests. And it came to pass, that, as they went, they were cleansed. And one of them, when he saw that he was healed, turned back, and with a loud voice glorified God." (full story: Luke 17:11–19)
Isa. 55:8–9	"For my thoughts are not your thoughts, neither are your ways my ways, saith the Lord. For as the heavens are higher than the earth, so are my ways higher than your ways, and my thoughts than your thoughts."
James 5:16	"confess your faults [or troubles] to one another and pray one for another, that ye may be healed. The effectual fervent prayer of a righteous man avails much."
Heb. 13:5b	"I will never leave or forsake you,"
1 Cor. 13:12	"For now we see through a glass darkly; but then face to face; now I know in part; but then shall I know even as also I am known."

Printed in the United States
by Baker & Taylor Publisher Services

Printed in the United States
by Baker & Taylor Publisher Services